A Christmas Eve Wish

By Nicole Dennis

Table of Contents

Escaping complications, hotshot chef Logan McNair rides his motorcycle into the middle of a blizzard and a cabin ruined by his younger brother's partying. At his wit's end, he sees the lights of a snowmobile come to his rescue. It's his neighbor, carpenter Joel Oliver, checking on the cabin and reporting more bad news. The road closed. Logan's stuck.

With the cabin uninhabitable, Joel offers him a place to stay for the Christmas holiday since the local inn is book solid. While Logan creates meals, he falls back in love with cooking, something he thought he lost. He also agrees to a Christmas fling as a present to each other.

Finding a lover who accepts him as plain Logan and not chef Logan is wonderful and thrilling. Could this only add to his complications? Or could loving Joel be finding the way back to himself?

The author acknowledges the trademarked status and owners of the following word marks used in this story:
Harley CVO Softail Convertible: *Harley-Davidson, Inc.*
Swiss Army Knife: *Swiss Army Brand, Inc.*
iPod: *Apple Inc.*
Boy Scouts: *Boy Scouts of America*

Chapter 1

The brilliant idea to take a ride on his motorcycle under sunny skies started out wonderful, it became idiotic when clouds rolled across the sky. They turned a dark gray and were heavy with snow.

After finishing the last of the holiday taping, Logan McNair raced out of the studio. He disappeared on his motorcycle without saying a word to anyone about his schedule or whereabouts. His life had become complicated. This was his chance to uncomplicate things. He took off on a ride to freedom from the monstrosity that had become his life. Unfortunately, for him, the drive took him headfirst into an oncoming blizzard.

Dressed in jeans, his favorite pair of boots, gloves, a worn padded leather jacket, and a helmet to protect his noggin, Logan wasn't dressed for this type of weather. His toes and fingers chimed in first with the tingling sensations of the beginning stages of hypothermia. The pleasant mind-clearing ride turned into a nightmare. Still, he couldn't stop in the middle of nowhere. He forced himself to continue until he reached the one hideaway left from his busy life— his small cabin placed outside the quiet town of Windy Valley, known for its gorgeous mountain lake and ski slopes. Leaning into the final bend, cautious of the snow, he knew this was the last curve to the cabin. He stopped the Harley CVO Softail Convertible directly in front of the door.

The headlight peered through the falling snowflakes and growing gloom.

Swinging his leg over, Logan jumped up and down, beat his hands on his legs and chest to get the blood flowing. He pushed the face-shield up and went to the door. Groaning when his numb fingers couldn't flick open the specially designed hide-a-key, he pulled off the helmet. His hands weren't nimble enough inside the thick leather gloves.

"Holy crap, its freezing."

Shoving the helmet under one arm, he used teeth to tug off the glove only to flick open the small log piece to find it was empty. "What the hell?" Dropping to his knee, Logan brushed at the snow to reveal the hiding spot for his backup key, and lifted the rug. Only to curse when he saw nothing but a dead spider. "Shit!"

Trudging through the snow, he rubbed an arm against the window and peered inside. The inside was in a ramshackle state. The sofa was in a different place, debris everywhere, no firewood, dishes piled by the sink, and a layer of dust covered everything. The set-up told him everything he needed to know about the culprit who invaded his private space.

"Mal! You little piece of shit! I'm going to wring your neck." Logan stomped around, praying there was propane and gas in the containers to give him heat. Perhaps a stack of firewood remained in the back. Reaching the back, he checked both containers to find them dry and twigs in the reserved stack.

"You're so dead, you piece of shit for a brother."

Teeth chattering, Logan moved to the back door and opened his Swiss Army Knife to the blade. Wiggling the blade and the handle, he heard the lock pop and grinned. The door swung open and he was inside. He kicked the door closed.

Okay. Inside. Out of the damn blizzard.

Moving to the front door, he went back out to remove the detachable saddlebags, the secured backpack from the passenger seat, and turned off the headlight. Removing a flashlight from the backpack, he flicked it on and returned inside.

He closed the door with another kick of his boot, set the bags and helmet on the table, and surveyed the damaged his dense little brother and friends had caused to his hideaway. Nearing the sofa, a sniff told him it was ripe with beer, cigarettes, and old sex. He cringed at the thought of an orgy going on in here. One look in the bedroom confirmed the drunken orgy-fest. He slammed the door shut and waved a hand in front of his nose. Then, he nearly puked at the disaster of the bathroom and resealed it with a slam of the door. He placed a hand on the wall until he got the nausea under control.

"Holy crap, that's ripe."

Shaking his head, he ventured into the kitchen, his pride and joy. Only to find all the cupboards empty, the trashcan filled with every imaginable type of fly and maggot, and empty liquor bottles and cans.

"Oh, gross."

Bright lights flickered through the windows and a roar of a snowmobile.

"What the—?" Moving to the backdoor, he opened it in time to see the rider, dressed proper in a full snowsuit, get off with a powerful flashlight in hand.

"Who is that? You're on private property," the rider called out.

Logan raised a hand to block some of the beam until the man lowered it a touch. "Yeah, this is my property. Who are you?"

"New neighbor on the lake. I'm going around the lake to check in on everyone before the blizzard hits full force. Not sure if anyone told you, but there was a bunch of crazy partiers here about two weeks ago. Called the cops on them and they fled, but nothing's been done to find them." The man trudged through the increasing snowdrifts, lowering the flashlight when he reached the back patio. He lifted the goggles to reveal lake blue eyes in the dim lights and unwound the thick scarf that protected his lower face and neck.

Logan shoved his hand through his hair and cursed under his breath. "That would be my idiotic younger brother, Malcolm, and his so-called friends. No, he doesn't have the right to be here. This place belongs only to me." He stepped back to let his neighbor inside to see the disaster.

"Shit, what the hell did they do?" The man went through the main area to take in the entire scene. "Looks like a damn crime scene."

"Trashed my place and had themselves a good old time. I have no idea exactly what happened and part of me doesn't want to know the details. All I want to do is wring the little bastard's neck."

"Gas and firewood?"

"Both are out. Same with food. I'm sure the pipes are frozen."

"There's no way you can stay here. An updated forecast came in before I left to check everyone."

"Shit, what's the damage? I've never seen it this bad up here."

"Blizzard will be overhead for at least four days, definitely through Christmas. Highway patrol shut down the pass out of here about fifteen minutes ago. You can't make it over unless you have a four-wheel drive."

Logan cursed under his breath. "Motorcycle."

The man's brow winged up. "You rode up here on a motorcycle? In a blizzard?"

"It was hot and sunny where I left and I didn't catch the forecast. Last minute decision on my part. I didn't expect a damn blizzard to blow in like this one."

The man chuckled. It turned into full out belly laughter as his hand waved around the cabin. After a desultory look around the place, Logan couldn't help but join in the laughter until his stomach hurt.

When they finished, Logan held out his hand. "Logan McNair."

"Good to meet you, Logan. I'm Joel Oliver." Pulling off the thick gloves, Joel placed his hand in Logan's and shook them.

Though his hands were still cold, Logan felt a delicious tingle of awareness and arousal at the touch. Joel's hand was comfortably calloused, not overbearing in the shake, with just enough pressure. The fingers were well shaped and long. The nails cared for and manicured. A warm woodsy smell accompanied him.

Logan gave the other man another look-over, with more attention to the finer details. There was the snow-damp, disheveled brown hair, which stood up in all directions around the goggles. The handsome face with deep lake blue eyes surrounded by thick lashes, well defined cheekbones, and great lips.

After being such a known star and celebrity, Logan found it hard to find someone who wasn't looking to fuck a TV star. Did Joel even know who he was? From the introduction, Logan couldn't tell.

"Well, Logan, to be flat-out honest. Your bike will not get through the pass."

"Yeah, I figured that part out. It was too late to turn around and return where I came from so I continued to drive here. I thought I would be fine, but now—" Logan dragged fingers through his auburn hair and looked around the cabin. "I'm pretty well in the fuck-you-idiot category."

"Don't even think about trying to fix this disaster. You don't have the time. This blizzard is too dangerous to mess around with your life. You can't stay here without food, water, or a heat source," Joel said, slapping his gloves against his thigh.

"That bad of a storm?"

"Did I mention it lasting through Christmas? Maybe longer than five days?"

Logan cursed a blue streak. "I guess I better get my ass down to the inn and snag a room."

"I doubt that will be a possibility. Not unless you buy out the inn or if you're some kind of celebrity."

Logan raised an eyebrow. Joel didn't know his name or face. "Why not?"

"You're definitely not from the valley, are you?"

"L.A.. Is it that obvious?"

"No, no, just a little funny how you said it." Joel held up a hand and shook his head. "It's Christmas. They're booked solid, been so for months. Unless you want to sleep in the lobby on one of the sofas."

Rubbing a hand against his neck, Logan knew he could drop his name and offer his skills in the kitchen for a room, but that would be harsh. He wouldn't do that, especially around the holidays, publicity or not.

"Damn, I'm sorely screwed. I'm going to kill my brother, slowly," Logan growled, kicking the back of the damaged sofa.

"Stay with me."

Logan twisted and stared at Joel. "What?"

"Answer to the problem," Joel said. "Stay at my cabin. I have the room, food, and don't mind the company."

"I'm a complete stranger."

Joel shrugged.

"Could be a killer on the run."

Joel snorted around a grin. "I can handle myself, and I doubt that."

"Worth a shot of warning. I'm only checking your sanity level."

"You're the one who rode up here on a motorcycle in a blizzard and you're checking *my* sanity level?"

Logan ran a hand over his neck. "Yeah, ironic piece of shit, isn't it?"

"We're running out of time. We need to get back to my cabin before the snow gets any deeper. Are you coming along?"

"Don't seem to have any other choice. How are we doing this?"

"I'm sure you don't want to leave your motorcycle here, correct?"

"Definitely correct in that assumption, she's my baby."

Joel moved to the front window and glanced at Logan's bike. "And a pretty girl at that, I don't blame you for not leaving her behind." He tapped his hand on the window and turned to face Logan. "Follow me back to my place. It's down the path and up the ridge."

"Through the woods to grandmother's house?"

"Smartass, huh?"

"Couldn't resist."

"To the carpenter's house, if you want the truth." Joel held up a hand to stop Logan from asking questions. "If you follow the tracks of the snowmobile, you should be fine. Do you have anything warmer around here to wear? A snowsuit or something?"

"I wasn't expecting it to snow. From what I could tell with my initial assessment, they damaged everything in their psychotic path. I have to replace everything but the cabin."

"Ahh. Shouldn't it be your brother replacing the damages, not you?" Joel asked.

Logan snorted. "You don't know Mal."

"We'll talk about that later." Joel glanced outside again. "Okay. We need to move. We're running out of time."

"Great! Time to freeze the nuts again. Can you get frostbite on your cock?"

"I'm sure we can prevent that from happening. We'll get you warm again at the cabin. Just follow me. I'll wait until you bring the bike around before leaving."

Logan shoved the flashlight into his backpack and zipped it before slinging the straps over his shoulder. He wouldn't bother reattaching it, just the saddlebags. He pulled on his gloves, then his helmet before picking up the saddlebags, and dug out his key. "I'll go out front and meet you in back. Don't bother locking. Just pull it shut hard. Not like anyone will want to steal this crap."

Doing the same with his hood, scarf, goggles, and gloves, Joel nodded.

Stepping out the front door, Logan shuddered hard at the freezing temperature. Joel was right, the weather was definitely turning worse and they couldn't stay outside for long.

Rushing to the bike, Logan reattached the saddlebags and straddled the seat. Pushing the key in the ignition, he gave the engine some gas and flicked the clutch with his boot. The powerful engine rumbled and roared between his legs.

"Thank you, baby, I'll get you safe in a few minutes. Just get me through this storm," he said to the bike, promising her the world.

Flipping down the visor, he kicked up the stand and rode around the cabin until he saw Joel and the snowmobile.

Chapter 2

After Joel raised a hand to acknowledge him, they took off through the snow down a hidden trail along the lake, passed trees, covered rocks, and toward the ridge. As long as he stayed in Joel's path, the motorcycle stayed somewhat smooth and in traction. Still, he froze in the wind, and it only became worse as the ride continued.

He barely noticed the cabin when they pulled in under the small carport. He shivered so hard, fumbled the key out of the ignition, and shoved the kickstand down. Swinging his leg over, he shoved gloved hands into his armpits. His teeth chattered inside the helmet.

Joel took care of something over by the snowmobile. He picked up a pile of fabric and returned to Logan's side. He set the pile aside and pulled off Logan's helmet. "Damn, you're worse off than I thought. I didn't think you would get so bad. Damn, I'm sorry for this. Let's get you inside. How do I unlock the saddlebag?"

"S-s-s-snap latch... f-f-f-front... b-b-b-b-back..."

"I'll figure it out. Door is open. Try to get out of your wet clothes in the mud room."

"S-s-s-sure?"

"Go inside, Logan, unlike you, I'm protected from this weather."

"M-m-m-my b-b-b—"

"I have an insulated protective cover. Go inside," Joel insisted with a gentle push.

Nodding, Logan shuffled to the door. A few fumbles with the handle and he stepped inside the mudroom. A long sigh of relief at the rush of heat against his numb skin escaped him. He managed to use his chattering teeth to tug off the gloves. His fingers had turned bright red and white with the beginnings of frostbite. Trying to curl them toward his palm, he cringed at the feeling of icicles ripping through the muscles and nerves, but they moved. He felt grateful for that bit of movement. His hands and fingers were his life. Without the dexterity within them, he couldn't cook. Losing the ability to cook meant the possible loss of the TV show and his career.

Would that be a bad thing?

At this point, Logan was tired of cooking for an audience he couldn't interact with or talk about his process and ideas. He talked to a damn camera lens and hoped someone would listen on the other side.

With all that racing in his head, Logan pushed it aside. He needed to get warm. He used his knuckles to grip the zipper of his leather jacket. Once he managed to pull it down, he shrugged out of it. Catching it in time, he hung it from a peg to let the leather drip dry. This left him in a damp white button-down shirt, a t-shirt, frozen jeans and boots. His treasured silver pendant hung on its leather strap around his neck. On one side, was a Celtic labyrinth and the opposite side had the universal symbol of gay pride stamped into the metal. He sat hard on a stool when the door opened.

Within a flood of snowflakes, Joel stepped inside with his bags. "Hey, need some help?" He set the bags down by the interior door.

"M-m-m-my hands hurt," Logan said.

Taking off his own gloves, goggles, hood, and scarf, Joel held Logan's hands and inspected them with care. He brushed his thumbs over the reddened fingers, frozen from the snow. "Looks like the initial stages of frostbite, but we have time to reverse it without damage to the nerves."

"I need my hands. M-m-m-my l-l-l-l—" Logan grumbled in frustration when he couldn't finish the words.

"I understand. I do. Hang in there. We'll fix you up. Let's get these jeans and boots off. We'll get you in front of the fire and wrapped in blankets."

"F-f-f-freezing..."

Joel placed Logan's hands on his lap and rubbed his hands hard on Logan's arms. "Stay with me, Logan. I'll warm you back up. Just focus on me."

"I'm... s-s-s-s-such... an... idiot... for... c-c-c-c-coming... here... Not... ch-ch-ch-checking..." Logan shook his head while his teeth chattered harder. His arms went around his body as he bent over himself. "C-c-c-c-cold. R-r-r-really... cold..."

"I know, Logan. I know."

Joel made quick work of Logan's boots, stripped off the socks, and rubbed the red and white feet between his hands.

"Ow! H-h-h-h-hurts!" Logan tried to pull his foot from Joel's grasp as the pins-and-needles feelings increased in a painful sensation.

"I know it hurts, but that's a good sign. It means the frostbite didn't penetrate to the muscles. Let me work through the pain." Joel moved to the other foot and did the same painful rubbing.

Logan felt ashamed when tears breached his eyes at the sensations rushing through his abused body. He had never hurt so much in his life. He saw Joel rise and shimmy out of the full-length snowsuit and boots. A murmur of appreciation rumbled in his chest at the revelation of a broad chest in the snug navy wool sweater and turtleneck and those long legs covered in simple warm tan corduroys.

"Hey, it's all right." Joel brushed Logan's hair away from his forehead.

"H-h-h-hit me... s-s-s-s-sudden..." Logan said.

Joel captured the swinging pendant and dropped his gaze to study the labyrinth. He rubbed his thumb over the imprint. "Beautiful craftsmanship."

"F-f-f-f-family... homeland... connection..." Logan whispered. "Other side...too."

Joel flipped it and lifted a brow at the symbol. A beautiful smile curved his lips. "This will make things much easier. Are you single?"

"Y-y-y-yes," Logan said, licked his lower lip. "You?"

"I am. You have good timing."

Logan snorted. "F-f-f-f-for freezing my nuts?"

Joel laughed hard and short. "Not particularly that part of the deal. We need to get these frozen pants off your tight ass." Placing a kiss on the gay side of the pendant, Joel released it, unsnapped and zipped Logan's jeans. He helped Logan rise to his feet. "Up you go, come on, you need to get the blood flowing."

Logan moaned in pain while he stood. Piercing sensations raced through his legs. "Hurts real b-b-b-bad."

"I know, but remember that's a good thing. Trust me in this." Joel worked the frozen denim over Logan's hips and long legs. "Hmm, black silk boxers. I like them."

Snorting in disbelief at the man's joke at this time, Logan shook his head, but ended shaking his whole body. Another shudder of cold ripped through his body. He closed his eyes and groaned again.

Rising, Joel made quick work of undoing the button-down shirt and tugged it off. This time, his thumb rubbed the Celtic armband tattooed around Logan's left biceps. Then he moved his hand down the simple T-shirt.

"You definitely didn't dress for the weather, crazy man."

"Th-th-th-that... sure... right," Logan said.

"Let's get you warm."

"I l-l-l-l-like the s-s-s-sound of that."

After digging through a basket, Joel yanked out a blanket. He shook it out and bundled Logan inside the warm folds. Then he wrapped an arm around Logan's waist and guided him out of the mudroom.

Logan noticed the kitchen off to the side and the large central room dominated by the stone covered fireplace. The built-in bookcases filled ceiling to floor with books on either side of the stones. When they moved around a loveseat, there was a mattress on the floor, covered in thick blankets, waiting for a body to nestle in its warmth.

"Waiting... f-for... someone?"

"Me."

"Huh?"

"I always bunk in the central room during blizzards and close up the outer rooms to conserve heat. Here, let me help you down close to the fire." Joel shifted his hold to help Logan sit. He tossed aside the first blanket.

"Hey..."

"This one is warmer." Joel enclosed Logan in a fire-warmed blanket, tucked in the ends to lock in the warmth.

Logan moaned when the warmth sunk into his skin.

"I'll be right back."

Continuing to moan with pure pleasure, Logan leaned forward and held his hands toward the fire's warmth. He shoved his feet in front and wiggled his toes. The flickers of warmth infiltrated the numb skin.

Busy trying to get some feeling back in his extremities, he barely noticed when Joel left him to enjoy the fire, and returned.

The mattress dipped next to him. Joel returned with a smile, dressed in a pair of sweatpants and t-shirt, and pressed a warm mug into his hands.

"Here, drink this." He helped Logan take hold of the heavy ceramic.

"What is it?"

"Simple chicken broth, warmed. Had it on the stove for me after my circuit around the lake."

"Does a body good." A smile curved his lips, before he raised the mug and sipped. His eyes drifted close as the heated liquid moved down his throat, warming him from the inside out, as the fire's heat tried to accomplish the opposite. "Did you finish all of your checking on the others?"

"Yeah, your place was last cause it was closest to mine."

"That was close?"

"For up here, yup." Joel shifted and rested his hands against Logan's back and chest under the blanket.

Opening his eyes, Logan blinked slow and watched him. "What... doing?"

"Your inner core temperature. I don't want it to drop." Joel let him finish the broth before he took the mug and set it on a nearby table. He pulled off his t-shirt and helped Logan out of his. Under the blanket, he shimmied out of the sweatpants and tossed them aside.

"What?"

"Curl up against me."

"Okay." Logan wiggled until his back pressed against Joel's front. A sigh left him at how it felt snuggling against someone. Joel was so warm against his cold body.

"I have you. I'll warm you, sleep in my arms," Joel whispered. He spooned Logan's body, tucked his arm tight around Logan's waist to bring them as close as possible. He moved his legs between Logan's to distribute the warmth, covering all of his skin.

"Hmm... not... tired..." Logan let out a long yawn.

"Yeah, right, you're not tired. You had a rough evening. Fall asleep. Let your body warm up and heal. I don't mind if you crash on me. This time I'll forgive you, next time you better be ready." The last few words all but purred. They caused the blood to sing in in a good way through Logan's veins.

"Hmm. Better keep that promise." Logan yawned hard, snuggled further back against Joel, if it was even possible. He wanted the barrier of their boxers removed but knew better than to ask. At least for tonight. With Joel's biceps as his pillow, Logan closed his eyes and let slumber pull him away.

Chapter 3

Curled against smooth skin, hard muscle, and long limbs, Logan didn't want to awaken from this wonderful dream. It's been so long since anyone joined him in bed, let alone slept all night. His muscles ached, but not in the after sex way. This was a harsh kind of ache. Not to mention the sheets felt different from his high thread-count cotton.

Still, there were strong arms holding him while he slept. He wiggled around to press chest to chest, swung his leg around and climbed closer to the other man's warmth. He was definitely a snuggler. His morning erection pressed against the silk boxers and not his lover's skin. This silky difference pulled him out of the deep sleep.

Logan blinked open. He rubbed one side of his face against his shoulder. Then he looked around his surroundings. This definitely wasn't what he expected. There was a large wooden coffee table and chocolate brown leather sofa. For some odd reason, they were on the ground. The lingering embers of a fire slumbered within the massive fireplace behind him.

Knuckling his eyes, Logan studied the powerful chest he'd slept on for most of the night. A very comfortable pillow.

A light mat of maple brown curls covered the upper curve of pectorals and disappeared until they appeared in the fold of the blankets. Even with the fireplace, the air was much too cool for Logan to raise the blankets. He lifted his admiring gaze up the collarbones and wide shoulders. His partner continued to sleep, undisturbed by Logan's movements. Morning growth of a beard covered the lower face but didn't hide the elegant jawline, masculine lips, and high cheekbones. Dark fans of lashes rested against his cheeks while matching brows arched across his forehead. Lifting his gaze higher, he enjoyed the maple sugar brown hair in an endearing messy style.

Logan grinned at how beautiful this man was in repose. Everything from yesterday hit him. Including everything about this man. His savior from the blizzard.

Joel.

A simple earthy name for this charming stranger. Joel Oliver. Under those long lashes lay clear lake blue eyes that held a world of secrets and desires. Both of which Logan wanted to learn and explore.

Other needs made their demands known. The fire was one of them and top on Logan's mental list.

Logan extracted himself from the warmth and snuggle buddy. He cocooned himself in a blanket while he snatched logs and shoved them into the huge pit. Then he poked the embers to wake them up into greedy flames. After seeing the young flames creeping around the fresh wood, he went in search of the bathroom.

Finding it on the far side of the fireplace and a short hallway, he shivered when he stepped inside. He left the door cracked open to let in the warmth. He grimaced at the grizzly image of himself in the mirror. A morning beard covered his lower face. Dark shadows were under his eyes. His face remained pale from yesterday's ordeal. He stared down while he carefully opened and closed each hand and then tested each finger. All of the strength and dexterity returned to them.

"Definitely not a good look for you, my man." He shifted blanket and boxers to take care of the morning call.

After cleaning what he could, he discovered his backpack and saddlebags in the mudroom and pulled them through an opening. He carried them closer to the fireplace. The backpack went on the loveseat. He took care setting it down because it carried his chef's knives and other personal items. Then he settled carefully on the mattress, trying not to disturb Joel. The saddlebags sprawled on the floor in front of him.

Glancing over his shoulder, he checked on Joel, who continued to sleep. Remembering everything Joel did for him yesterday, he wanted the man to sleep as long as he could. There was a way to thank his snowy angel for everything. That is if the kitchen's appliances were running. Grinning, Logan scrounged in the saddlebags to locate a pair of jeans, cotton boxers, socks, a thermal undershirt, and a cotton button-up shirt. Trying to keep the noise down, he slid off the mattress and onto the rug. Then he wiggled into the clothes under the blanket. He grabbed his razor kit and toothbrush and returned to the bathroom.

Minutes later, feeling better, his lower face clean-shaven and teeth defuzzed, Logan pulled his chef's kit and iPod from the backpack. He went to the massive kitchen filled with silver matte appliances and heavy granite countertops.

Clipping the iPod on his jeans, he placed the wireless headset over his head and found a morning playlist to energize him. Seeing one, he chose it and hit the play button. Murmuring the words under his breath, his hips moved to the pumping beat, he grinned at the choice of song.

Setting down the leather roll-up kit, Logan untied and unrolled it to reveal the gleaming knives, perfectly balanced to his arm length, hands, and skill, on the granite countertop. Running his fingers along the countertop in admiration of the beauty of the well-designed kitchen, he rummaged through all the cabinets, the pantry, and the various top-end appliances to familiarize himself. He admired the beauty and artisanship of the woodwork. Joel mentioned being a carpenter and Logan wondered if he was looking at his work now. Finding the coffee, he set up a pot to brew in the coffeemaker. He went to work whipping up a fabulous pancake breakfast with bacon and crispy seasoned potatoes for his sleeping companion.

The delicious aroma of coffee, bacon, potatoes, and pancakes filled the cabin. The scents pulled Joel out of a deep sleep. Blinking the sleep out of his eyes, he shifted himself up on his elbows. One glance told him he was alone on the mattress. Logan wasn't next to him, but there were signs he remained close. The fire stirred with new logs. The saddlebags and backpack rested on the loveseat after he left them in the mudroom. Logan obviously went through them.

Rolling to the side, Joel grabbed the shirt and sweatpants he'd discarded and dressed. Then he rose to look toward the kitchen.

Logan danced. Smooth and graceful, he glided from one area to the next. A bright purple headset covered Logan's ears.

Joel stepped into his favored sheepskin-lined slippers warmed in a nook by the fireplace and went to the nearest bedroom. He yanked off the T-shirt and replaced it with a thermal undershirt and a heavy Irish knit sweater. Then he went to the bathroom where he noticed Logan added his toiletries kit on the counter. He touched the extra razor and toothbrush handle with a smile. There was a comfortable hominess to the appearance of their things mixing. A glance in the mirror revealed the sappy smile.

After he made quick work of his morning routine, he made his way back to the kitchen and braced a shoulder against the fridge. There, he watched a very different Logan from the one he met yesterday. The one who stood crestfallen and dejected, shivering down to his bones, in a ramshackle cabin. This one was full of confidence and self-assuredness while he flipped perfect pancakes and diced potatoes on the griddle while keeping a careful eye on the bacon. All the time, he rocked to whatever music played on the bright purple iPod clipped to his tight-fitting jeans and wireless headset. He slid along the floor in his socks during different moves, but it helped him get from the oven, to the counter, and back.

Grinning, Joel noticed the coffeemaker was full and ready. Two mugs set next to it. He needed a hit of caffeine. There was the lure of that tight ass calling for a slap of a hand. His hand wanted to be on that ass.

"Choices. Choices."

Shuffling into the kitchen, Joel sidled behind Logan and took choice number two.

He slapped that tight rear end.

"Whoa! What?" Logan shouted, almost bobbled the pancake. He turned and grinned. "Hey!"

Not moving his hand from the ass, Joel cupped and gripped the taut cheek. "Nice butt. Loved the way you wiggled it."

"Pardon?"

Chuckling, Joel slipped one side of the headset away from Logan's ear. "I said nice butt. You wiggle it pretty good when you're getting down to the groove."

Pulling the head set off, Logan turned off the music. He placed the iPod and headset on a counter out of his way. "Thank you. It was some fine music. I do love me some Luke Bryan. Gorgeous man and equally awesome voice."

"Country music. Didn't expect that from a L.A. man."

"Grew up in Texas before I ventured out to California. Got country music in my blood."

"Why the change?"

"Small town where religion ruled and gays weren't welcomed. I couldn't follow my dreams there and I wouldn't change to fit in their ideals and morals."

"Good reason."

Logan shrugged.

Joel poured a cup of coffee from the pot. Breathing in the delicious scent, he took a long sip. "Hmm. You brewed a nice pot."

"I didn't want to wake you since you were sleeping so soundly. After all the help you gave me yesterday, I figured you could use the rest. I hope I wasn't noisy," Logan said.

"No, the aroma was a wonderful invitation. I enjoyed the unusual wake-up call."

"This is how I make myself welcome whenever I'm a guest in someone's home. I invade their kitchen."

"You're welcome to invade throughout your stay then, since it seems you know your way around. Far better than me at any rate."

"I didn't expect to find all of this beauty and high-end equipment in a log cabin, other than my place. Do you use it?"

"Not too much. I can do basics, but when I renovated the place I went full out."

"Go big or go home."

"Something like that," Joel said. He grinned behind the mug at Logan's dry sense of humor and his little misplaced zingers.

Logan swished the spatula around to encompass the kitchen. "You're well stocked for the blizzard."

"I had an extra delivery for the holiday. The weather started to look bad so I decided to order a little more than my usual. We'll be fine."

"I've made do with far less. Go and sit, I'll bring everything over." Logan shifted closer and brushed his lips against Joel's cheek.

Joel leaned back and stared at Logan.

"Too forward?"

"No. Unexpected, but no."

"Good."

Joel swept his lips against Logan's mouth and captured Logan's lips in a welcoming kiss. Their kiss was warm and soft. Their lips malleable while they tasted one another, tested each other.

Logan sighed when the kisses separated into short, slow kisses. He stepped back and drew his fingers down Joel's jaw. "Hmm, I definitely enjoyed that."

"Same here. Can't wait for more."

"Go and sit for breakfast. We'll explore more of this later."

After a delicious breakfast, Joel gathered the dishes and carried them back to the kitchen. He studied the slight mess left behind by his guest and noticed some of the ingredients out on the counter. Logan created the pancakes from scratch and not from the large bag mix.

"Those were scratch pancakes?"

Logan walked in with the platter and scooped the leftovers in storage containers. "Of course, I don't use mixes if I can help it. You never know what is in those things. I suffer from a sensitive gastro system. It's better for me to control the ingredients. I shouldn't be eating the bacon, but to hell with it. After yesterday, I damn well deserved it."

"It's damn good bacon."

Logan chuckled and nodded. "Exactly. I can't resist my own cooking."

"Did you go to school for this?"

"This is one of the dreams that drove me to get out of my hometown. I went to school, worked my way through restaurants on the various stations until I got to sous-chef and chef. Stayed at a top restaurant as head chef for a few years until I built up enough capital to open my own restaurant." Logan filled the sink with soap warm water and washed the pile of used dishes.

"How did it do?" Joel stacked the bowls and pans to add to the pile for Logan to wash. Then he wiped down the griddle, put it away, and snagged a wet cloth to wipe the counters.

"It's still a top place and highly recommended as one of the best places to eat in L.A., Chicago, Austin, and New York," Logan said with a grin. "I'm opening a few more in Seattle, Las Vegas, Boston, and Atlanta."

"Damn. I'm impressed."

Logan shrugged. "Nothing to be impressed about since I'm a chef who loves his job and giving people good stuff to eat. When you come to my restaurant, you'll enjoy a fulfilling meal. Plus, I ensure all the ingredients are all natural, organic if possible, and some of it locally grown to support the farmers and ranchers. Everything is made from scratch."

"Are you charging a ridiculous price for an ounce of food?"

"Hell, no," Logan said. He added a snort of disgust. "I'm not one of those chefs. I'm not stuck that far up my ass. If I am, someone better knock me back down to reality."

Joel laughed at the image Logan's words created in his head. "Guess I better check out one of your places. Perhaps, I'll see then if I need to give you one of those hard knocks. Especially since I don't want that fine ass ruined." He caught the saucy look Logan gave him.

"What is it with you and my ass?" Logan flicked his soapy fingers to send a spray of bubbles at Joel.

Brushing the soap off his shirt, he scrounged a towel from a drawer to attack the pile of wet dishes. "I saved it, so I want to take a chance."

"Take a chance?"

Joel tilted his head to study his guest. "With more than a kiss. Logan, we're both single."

"Hmm, so you mentioned."

"Then I'm requesting permission for us to enjoy a Christmas fling while you're here."

"A fling?"

"I know you don't live here, not permanently, so I won't ask for more. You have your life in L.A. while I have mine in the valley."

"I own a cabin here."

"You visit for what? A week at a time. Months pass between those visits."

"Well, yes, but—"

"After the holiday and the pass opens, you'll return your life and I'll go on with mine." Putting the towel down, dropping the pretense of drying dishes, he sidled closer, trailed a few fingers down Logan's arm.

Drying his hands, Logan turned to him. "What you're offering me then is we'll have a few days of hot sex. Then you'll let me walk away."

"Exactly. A Christmas gift to each other. A no strings and no promises affair."

"I can handle that."

"Good. Now to seal the deal—" Joel placed his mouth against Logan's lips for a kiss. He threaded his fingers through Logan's soft auburn hair, drawing him closer while the kiss deepened. When Logan's hands slid under his sweater, causing a moan to rise in his throat, he pulled back and let it out.

Logan leaned his forehead against Joel's head. Their heated breaths mingled. "About Christmas, Joel."

"Hmm... What about it?"

"There are no decorations in here. Doesn't feel very holiday-ish."

"We can change that. I have a tree in my workroom. I'm letting it get accustomed to the pail. The branches needed to unfurl."

"Wait." Logan waved around a hand to stop Joel. "You have a live tree?"

"Yeah, I'll show you. I don't like cutting them down. It pays to be nice to the environment around here."

Logan let out a low whistle.

"The tree should be ready. We can bring it inside along with the rest of the boxes."

"Workroom? What workroom?"

"It's set in the far back of the house, not seen from where we came in yesterday. I'm a carpenter and overall general contractor."

Logan looked around and pointed to him. "All the woodwork around here?"

Joel nodded.

"Cabinets?"

"Cabinets included."

"Damn, I thought you did them because they're far more customized than anything I can find online or in stores," Logan said while he ran his fingers down the closest upper cabinet. "It's truly beautiful work."

"Thank you. I used to do a lot of restoration and flipping houses, but ended up leaving the big city and moved here. Unlike other flippers who turned the profit into buying another house, I saved a large portion of each sale and tucked it into other investments to create a tidy nest egg. With such a meteoric rise of the housing prices and business, I predicted things would bottom out. There would be hundreds of people fighting to get the houses and flip them."

"By saving money, you looked beyond the time of flipping houses instead of dealing with the present or the next project."

"Bingo," Joel said with a nod. "It's what kept me afloat through the difficult time and got me here. I do odd jobs around town and for the hotel. Then I sell pieces online and various local boutique shops to bring in some income."

"What a trip this turn into for me. I can't wait to see your shop or you in action. I thought I smelled fresh wood when we met."

"I was in the shop before I went around the lake to check on everyone. Then I saw your headlight and flashlight and rushed over. After that group came through, I kept an eye on the place."

"Thanks for that. Damn my brother."

Joel wrapped his hand around Logan's neck, calmed him with his touch. "Forget him for now. You can handle him after the holiday."

"This wouldn't be the first time I cleaned one of his disasters," Logan said. "Doubt it will be the last. Only this time he did far more damage. I don't know if I can salvage anything from the cabin, even the cabin itself."

"Hey, hey." Joel trapped Logan within the corner against the countertop and cabinets. Using his hold on Logan's neck, he captured his gaze. "We'll deal with him later. Right now, it's about us. Okay? Push the trouble with your brother and cabin aside. This holiday is only us."

"You know how long it's been since I spent a quiet holiday? One where I could sit back, relax and actually enjoy the day with good friends and family."

Joel shook his head.

"Too damn long to even remember." Bracing his hands against the countertop behind him, Logan leaned back from Joel's grip enough for him to relax it just a bit. His gaze took on a distant appearance while he tried to remember a couple of fond memories of him, his brother and sister along with their parents on Christmas. Where there any decent memories he wanted to remember?

A soft smile curled his lips at the one memory of racing downstairs when he was barely six, in pajamas, hair tousled from bed, the house dark and quiet. His sister and brother cried out how Santa came when they found a big pile of toys around the tree. He received a play-set full of cookware that Christmas. It was odd for a boy, but his mother knew how much he loved being in the kitchen with her, helping her make food even back then. Perhaps his dream of being a chef truly started to take hold right at that moment.

"What are you thinking about?"

"A childhood Christmas when I was six. Got my first set of cookware. I played chef."

"That's a long time."

"Told you it was."

"Let's make this Christmas one we both will remember for years after."

Wrapping his own hand around Joel's neck, Logan smiled and kissed Joel. "Agreed. Dishes are done. Kitchen cleaned. Time to get the tree and decorations. We need to transform this place."

"You want to do all this right now."

"Hell yes. I have a yearning to decorate. Then we can curl up by the fire and sparkling lights."

"I like that idea. All right, then, follow me."

After bundling up in jackets and boots, Joel took Logan through the mudroom to a different door. It opened to a large airy room filled with windows highlighting the blizzard. Heavy gray clouds filled the sky between the surrounding mountains and continued to drop the heavy wet snowflakes on the valley and small village. For the most part, Joel didn't keep the heat on while working.

Inside, Joel carefully arranged top-notched machines around the floor, lined the walls with tools of all types, metal containers, and shelves filled with different lengths, cuts, and styles of woods. There were other stations for painting, staining, assembly, and drying.

"This is amazing." Logan walked over to a piece in the middle of construction. He crouched to check out the lines and beauty.

"Thanks."

"What are you making?"

"That is going to be a dining room hutch custom-made for a couple. I built them a dining table and chairs, now they want a hutch to match and a sideboard. It's one of the higher priced jobs I get from time to time."

Joel went to another corner and opened a door. Cold air blew in with snowflakes, but he dragged in a small old-fashioned washboard tub. He slammed the door shut.

"Damn, it's cold out there. Hope the tree didn't freeze. I thought I put enough water around it to protect the roots."

Logan walked over to see the beautiful five-foot pine. After so many years of fake trees, he almost forgot what a real pine tree looked and smelled like. It brought back the memories of that childhood Christmas, walking through the tree lot to choose their 'special' tree. Emily, Logan and Malcolm's little boots stomped through the snow, their small cheeks flushed red from the cold, with mittens full of snowballs they tossed at each other. Their parents went from one tree to the next to see if this was the one to bring home. At different ones, they asked them if this was 'their' tree. If it could become the tree that Santa Claus would place their presents underneath if they would remain good boys and girl.

He slid a few fingers down the long evergreen needles. The young tree shaped beautifully from top to bottom, a perfect triangle, nice and full. He could easily imagine what it would look like full of lights and ornaments. The tree stood tall and true in the tub. Crouching down, he looked in and saw the root ball intact covered in burlap. "I still can't believe you have a live Christmas tree."

"Every year I dig up a young one in the mountain and bring it down. Then I bury it back around the property," Joel said, touching the deep green needles. "I hate cutting down one of these beauties for a few weeks of enjoyment. A little extra work, but a lifetime of fresh air and pine scent."

Breathing in the fresh pine scent, Logan smiled. "Ahh, damn I love that scent. One of my favorite scents of the season. Let's bring it in. Where do we place it?"

"Large front window opposite the fireplace."

"Good spot. Each take a side?"

"Take it by the base and handle. It's heavier than it looks," Joel warned.

Taking their spots, Joel counted it off and they lifted together. They worked together to carry the tree inside to the main room and set it in front of the window.

"Oh damn, my aching back. That's a heavy tree all right." Logan pressed his hands against his lower back and stretched, groaning at the pain and ache. He stepped away and ordered Joel to center the tree until he was satisfied.

"Are you going to be like this throughout the decorating process?" Joel pulled in a few deep breaths, hands shoved on hips.

"It's Christmas. This is my first one I've decorated in a while. I'm damn sure going to make sure it will be perfect. So, yes."

"Wait a minute, your first one to decorate? What are you talking about?"

"Thanks to my job, things are complicated around the holidays."

"That's all you're going to give me."

"Right now, yes, please? I'll explain later but I don't want to ruin our holiday together," Logan said. "Could we get back to work? The tree isn't centered."

"Oh, sweet heaven, I'm in trouble."

"Only if you don't follow orders," Logan said with a grin. "Now, move the tree a few more inches to the left."

Laughing at his perfection and not moving the tree, Joel captured Logan's jacket and dragged him back to the workplace for the tubs of decorations stored under a workbench. He added a box of fresh-cut pine-tree boughs to place around the fireplace and other places for more greenery.

Within fifteen minutes, all five tubs were inside and opened. After removing the coats and replacing the boots with the slippers, Logan returned to the tubs to see what decorations Joel stored away.

"Want more coffee?" Joel offered.

"Please. Put on some Christmas music on your stereo system or we can hook up my iPod."

"I have music. Black coffee?"

"With two sugars. Do you prefer color or white lights?"

"The white lights, I don't have any more color lights in there," Joel said from the stereo system as he popped in CDs. He programmed the player and walked away when the music kicked on with the first song.

"They do have a gorgeous twinkle about them amongst the evergreen, don't they?"

"Hmm, definitely. Try not to curse during the de-tangling of the lights."

"Me? Curse? Now what kind of fellow do you think I am?"

Returning with two coffee mugs, Joel settled next to Logan smiled. "That's what I'm still figuring out."

"Where are the lights?"

"Ahh..." Joel got to his knees and peered into the tubs. "This one has the tree stuff. Lights and most of the decorations are in here." He pulled out the boxes of ornaments, ribbon, garland, and lights.

"Then that's the box we start with. Let's see what beauty and bounty you stored away for us to discover." After sipping from the coffee mug, Logan set it aside. He felt warm and cheery inside, the weight of his life in L.A. dissipating for a few hours while the holidays came into play.

There was plenty of inventive cursing filling the air. They tried to figure out the tangles of strings. Then the playful banter started.

It was mostly Joel defending his actions the previous year, and Logan explaining what he should've done to prevent such tangles in the first place. Either way, they ended up with laughter while Logan sent Joel shuffling to the nearest outlet to plug in each strand to test the lights.

"I prefer them blinking in unity." Logan cursed another small streak when the line yanked back around a nasty snarl of lights. "Damn, Joel, why did you neglect your poor lights? Do you do this to torture yourself every Christmas?"

"Nah, blinking lights are annoying as all hell. Let's leave the lights plain and non-blinking." Joel sat next to the plug so he wouldn't have to shuffle or rise every other minute to test the lights. "And would you stop your cursing and complaining about the wires?"

Moving his attention from the strands in his lap, Logan lifted his gaze to study Joel's simple actions, unplugging the latest strand after the test. He set it with the good ones. His body trembled at the sight of those delicious muscles shifting and flexing under the sweater and jeans. Licking his lips, he swallowed hard as he studied those ripples, wishing for less clothing. "Come on, that's boring."

"They never blink all the same time anyway. Not unless you have one of those funky timers, which I don't. So, no blinks. Pop out that red tipped thing and put in a regular bulb. My house, my decorations."

"So boring," Logan said, but did as ordered with the strand. He playfully tossed the newly released bulb at Joel.

There was another delightful shift and play of musculature under the sweater for him to enjoy vicariously when Joel caught the tiny bulb and set it aside.

"Yeah, yeah," Joel teased. "Shut it and give me the next strand."

"You mean the one you hopelessly tangled to death."

Joel raised his eyebrow. "Smartass is asking for something to happen to him."

"Ooh, I'm scared." Logan gave a playful shudder and laughed.

Pushing aside the lights, Joel growled and rolled to all fours. With a few quick movements and a near silent slide on the wooden floor, he rushed him.

Logan squirmed when Joel wrapped one hard arm around his waist. He felt himself flipped and flat on his back. Joel straddled his body, hands pushing his hands back to the floor. He wiggled his hips, but Joel locked his thighs around him.

"What the hell! Joel!" Logan tried to get free, but Joel leaned over and smacked a kiss on his lips.

A shot of pleasure and pain rushed through Logan. He moaned under the heated kiss attack and melted into the floor. His cock hardened against his zipper and pressed against Joel's erection.

Joel lifted his head and stared down at him.

"Holy shit!"

"Guess no one dared to kiss you into silence."

Logan shook his head. With his position on a favorite cooking show, no one dared talk back to him at all, let alone try to kiss him. While his position was demanding, it was also damn lonely.

"I'll have to keep that in mind. For next time?"

"Next time?" Logan squeaked. It was unmanly and his face reddened.

Joel laughed. He curled both of them to a sitting position, but kept the straddling position with Logan over him.

When Joel kissed him, Logan delved his fingers into Joel's hair, the short hairs at the nape, the longer locks near his ear and temple. The kiss deepened until they were breathless.

Joel brushed their lips together. "Are you going to behave?"

"Not if you keep punishing me like this."

"I think that can be arranged." Laughing, Joel helped him shift back to the floor before he moved to his former position.

Logan grumbled as he shifted into a different position to rearrange his swollen cock and tried to adjust his jeans.

Joel grinned when he caught sight of Logan's wiggling. "Having some trouble?"

"You caused all of it." Logan tossed him the end of another tangled strand of lights, watched Joel wink and grin.

Joel plugged it in to reveal a dead strand.

Logan clapped his hands once. "Hah, you're in luck. We don't have to untangle it."

"Dead pile. Damn, I need to restock my lights." Joel tossed the strand in the dead lights bundle and shook his head. "How many good strands do we have?"

Glancing over at the untangled strands, Logan counted, lips moving along with his finger. "We have ten. Two more strands to test."

"Let's finish testing then. See what we have."

Logan handed him the last two plugs and watched Joel plug in both at the same time. They grinned as both lit perfectly and neither blinked.

"Hah, lucked out on the last two. I'll unravel one, you get the other," Joel said, unplugging them.

"Damn these wretched things. The bane of every existence except for those with pre-lit trees."

"But they don't have fresh pine smell."

"True, true. But a snap here, snap here, plug in and done. Poof, the tree is up and ready to decorate."

"Boring. Same tree every year with the exact same placement of branches and ornaments. What's the fun in that?"

Tilting his hips a different way to relieve pressure on his cock, Logan grumbled when it didn't help. Again, he caught Joel's sideways grin at his discomfort. He desperately wanted to drag Joel over and arouse him to the point of madness. "Yeah, I guess." After finishing his strand first, he linked the strands together. He shoved the plug into the wall to keep them on to see them while winding the wires around the tree. "Get your butt up and start winding them around the tree, mister."

"Why me?"

Logan stuck up a finger and said, "One, you're taller than me so you can reach farther." Logan added a second finger. "Two, this is your house, your tree." A third finger went up. "Three, I don't do lights. I do ornaments."

Joel griped while he pushed himself to his feet. He accepted the end of the strand.

Standing with him, Logan fed him the remainder of the strands while Joel shifted and stepped around the tree. Together, they tucked, wove, and draped the lights through the branches.

"Nah, that row should be a branch higher. We have enough lights to put them on almost every row of branches," he instructed.

Joel gave him a distracted look.

"Please? Take your time and do it my way. It will look fabulous."

"Very well." He went back to re-drape the requested row.

Logan enjoyed the view of the tree lit to perfection in front of him. "Hmm, how beautiful. This part of the process is such a pain so they removed and simplified it with the fake ones, but took away the simple beauty of lighting a real tree. Of how you can highlight each branch, the curve of the needles, the shadows against the walls and ceiling. Soon the lights will warm the needles and bring out that rich pine aroma. Damn, I love this season. Why didn't I take the time to slow down and enjoy the holidays? I kept pushing myself harder and faster."

Opening his eyes after taking a deep breath, Logan stopped to see Joel staring at him. His hands cupped around a branch and lights. Those elegant lake blue eyes took on a dreamy look as his head tilted to the side.

"You're a poet, Logan."

"Nah, a simple chef."

"You underestimate yourself. You create poetry with food, why not with words?"

Settling the strand in the branches, Joel stepped over to him. Logan shifted his weight, tilted his head to keep his gaze on Joel's face. Joel leaned over just enough to kiss him.

Their lips brushed, softened, opened, and lingered.

Logan wanted to capture a taste of Joel to remember after their parting. One simple savor. He, who created various types of tastes from sweet, to sour, to savory, to tangy, to spicy for everyone who dined on his food, wanted to know what the taste of his lover reminded him of making. Cupping Joel's cheek, he deepened their kiss to sweep against Joel's sensitive palate.

Coffee. Savory. Lingering sweetness of maple sugar.

Perfection. Taste of Joel.

Logan brushed his lips against Joel's once and then twice more. He gave him another softer kiss. His thumb swept against the high cheekbone, before playing with the dent in Joel's chin.

"Hmm," Joel murmured, nearly purred under his attention. "Are you analyzing me like a new unknown dish?"

Logan pulled back in surprise. "How?"

"Don't underestimate yourself. Not with me, Logan. I will not let you." Joel tapped his nose with a finger. Rising, he returned to the tree.

Logan blinked twice, in pure amazement at Joel's sheer insistence and belief in his abilities. What does Joel see in him?

"There, the lights are done with enough give to reach the outlet. Did you find the angel in the box? Let me put him on top first."

"Him? A male angel?"

"Of course, it's a male angel. What would I want with a female one?"

Logan searched through the tub. Sure enough, when he opened it, the angel had a masculine face and mostly nude body with full white wings and a halo. He cracked up laughing and held it up. "Holy shit! Where did you find this?"

"One of my friends gave it to me. They found it in San Francisco during the holidays and said I needed a gay angel for my tree." Joel took the angel and nestled him against the top branches. He secured the legs onto the sturdiest ones to keep the angel in place.

"That is too damn perfect!"

"They got one for everyone at the party. Male homo angels and lesbian angels. I think there was even a transsexual angel."

"No way?"

Joel nodded.

Logan leaned back against the chair, laughing so hard he wrapped arms around his aching stomach. When he opened his eyes, Joel leaned over him and stared down with a bemused expression. Reaching out with both hands, Logan snagged hold of the sweater. Tugging him down, they rolled around the floor, lips crushed together while their legs tangled.

When he finally came up for breath, Logan used the back of his hand to prop his chin upon Joel's chest. His other fingers traced the lean hard line of Joel's jaw and stubborn chin. He followed the kiss-swollen lips with his forefinger.

"Are we decorating?"

"Hmm, each other?" Logan grinned.

Joel laughed.

Abandoning the tree for passion, they moved to the pile of mattress and blankets.

Letting Joel take over and pull him to a sitting position, Logan hummed when Joel's calloused fingers skimmed over his shoulders, down his chest, and felt for the hem on his thermal and T-shirt and tugged them both up. Then everything went dark with his hands stuck behind his head when Joel trapped him with his shirts pulled halfway off—just covering his eyes and ensnaring his hands.

"Joel?"

"Ssh... Just concentrate on feeling."

Cold air hit his lower body when Joel unbuttoned and dropped his pants and boxers in one go.

"Keep the socks. My toes are cold," Logan said.

Joel chuckled while he pressed kisses along Logan's belly. "Step out." He guided Logan with a touch along each calf.

Logan licked his lips as his breathing hitched while Joel kissed back up his body. He was guided back to lie with his head tilted back against the pillow, his sight darkened by the shirts. He moaned as Joel's lips traveled down the warm skin revealed by the shirts. No longer frozen from yesterday's ordeal, his skin was back to its normal golden tone. He felt a gentle tweak on the light covering of body hair around each flat nipple before a concentric series of circles traced around each nipple and pectoral. He twitched and wiggled at the light, airy sensation that ignited the nerves under the skin. Then a whiff of warm air blew over his nipple, tightening it to a taut bud before a tongue laved it. A moan escaped Logan's lips as the same series of movements were repeated on his other nipple.

Joel's warm hands moved down Logan's belly, caressing the rows of abdominal muscles before moving up his arms. One hand cupped his neck and their lips came together. Their lips parted and their tongues flicked together in the similar rhythmic way of lovemaking.

Joel pulled back and cursed under his breath. "Hang on a second. Not prepared for this," he said while he pushed away.

"What?" Logan wiggled against the confining shirt, unable to see.

"Forgot stuff. Be right back. Don't move."

"Yeah, right," Logan said back in the same light sarcastic tone.

Not knowing where Joel went, Logan felt time lingered and dragged while he remained in the dark. His body warmed by the fire, but missed Joel's heat.

"Okay. Now we're set."

When Joel joined him, Logan felt the expanse of warmed skin against his body. The harsh brush of clothes no longer there. A soft whoosh of air left him at the sensation.

Joel nuzzled along Logan's neck. "Doing okay?"

"Yeah, where did you go?"

"You'll find out."

When he tried to answer, Joel captured his mouth in another kiss. Logan moaned against Joel's mouth when he felt fingers against the tight, sensitive ring of his ass. When Joel stroked between Logan's cheeks and behind his balls, Logan tilted his hips up. The cold slickness of lube caused a twitch of muscles. He realized that's what Joel disappeared to get. Logan's cock jerked between them, and he groaned when Joel's fingers entered him, preparing him.

Logan's breath hitched again as he moaned. His teeth sank into his lower lip when he felt Joel lift and open his legs wider. Searing, toe curling pleasure-pain fired through his abdomen when a long massive shaft shoved into his well-lubricated hole. Logan whimpered at the intensity of having Joel inside him. His hands gripped the shirt behind his head.

"Breathe, lover mine. Breathe," Joel said.

Letting out a long, harsh breath, Logan arched his neck. His toes dug into the bed. "Let me see! I need to see you!"

"Relax, let me in first. Relax, Logan, open up to me."

Logan willed his body to loosen, his muscles to soften, and squeezed in reaction to the intrusion of Joel's sheathed cock. Logan lifted and shifted against Joel's movements, trying to make it easier for his lover to enter him. He felt the fullness turn sensual, more erotic, as it hit all those nerves. When the shaft slid all the way to the hilt, he wrapped his legs around Joel's thighs.

Finally, Joel removed the shirt, clearing Logan's sight and freeing his eyes, ears, and hands in one swoop. Logan closed his eyes, blinked a couple of times before focusing on the passion-darkened eyes of his lover while he was deep inside him. He grasped Joel's powerful shoulders with one hand, while the other cupped the back of his head. His fingers threaded through Joel's soft hair.

When he turned to press a kiss on one of the straining biceps, Logan felt Joel withdraw until only the head of his cock bumped the rim. Moving his hand from Joel's shoulder, he drew his fingers down the straining back, and gripped the curve of one ass cheek.

Slowly Joel began to move against him. He pressed forward, sliding the massive cock all the way in, the tip of his glans bumping the sensitive prostate, shooting all kinds of sensations through Logan's abdomen. Joel moved in and out, back and forth, each time sending jolts of pleasure through Logan's body. Joel steadily picked up the pace, moving faster and faster, creating more friction and pressure with every plunge.

Moaning, breathing, and groaning filtered the air, joining the Christmas carols.

Their lips smashed together as they exchanged heavy kisses in between gulping in breaths.

Logan let out a needy moan and gripped Joel's hips harder, smashing his cock between their stomachs. Logan's head arched back over the pillow. He felt Joel lave kisses down his neck before nipping on his collarbone. The pressure mounted in his balls and knotted his cock.

"Please, I'm going to come, Joel."

"Same here, same here." Joel tilted himself, gripped Logan's cock in his hand and began squeezing, tightening, and pulling on Logan's hard cock.

Jerking and thrusting, Logan cried out with relief. Spurts of milky cum shot from his cock and splashed across his belly then Joel's belly and hand. He continued the long, hard orgasm when he felt Joel tumble over the edge.

When Joel lowered himself for a kiss, they met in a near desperate need for one another as shudders raced through their bodies. The sensations lingered between them.

Chapter 6

Content, Logan's body sated from Joel's tender care. Logan hummed to the Christmas carol while he placed the various ornaments on the tree's branches. The ornaments were a beautiful collection of intricately carved wooden pieces Joel created over the years mixed in with silver and gold ones he picked up during his travels. It went beautifully with the plain silver and gold garland they draped.

Picking up a delicate reindeer, Logan cradled it to stare at the intricate antlers. It was amazing, even down to the strands of fur Joel picked out in the wood, the hooves, a harness of bells, and the simple paintwork. He flipped it over and saw the same detail on the opposite side, perfectly matching.

"My God, Joel, this is gorgeous! How long do these ornaments take to create?"

"The reindeer? Each one took a few hours for the carving once I had the pattern. The detailing takes longer, but the painting is simpler. Then I put a glaze over it to protect everything from wear and tear. Rudolph should be somewhere in the box. I have all nine of them."

"Do you sell these?"

"At the hotel's shop during the holidays and the local boutique shop in town. There's a big arts and crafts fair in a nearby valley that runs in the fall. I participate in it if I have enough inventory. Brings in a decent crowd and the payoff is enough to make it worth the trip."

"It's good some people still respect craftsmanship when they see it," Logan said.

Joel leaned out from his place and grin. "Thank goodness for that or I would truly be in trouble."

It didn't take much long for Logan to empty the box and hang all the ornaments. He placed his hands on hips while studying the tree.

Joel moved to join him, slid his arm around Logan's waist. "What do you think?"

"Beautiful. What else do you have?"

"Fresh garland for the mantel along with a wooden Santa and reindeer set and some more carvings for the bookcases and branches. I keep it fairly simple."

"How about I start dinner and you finish up?"

"Sounds like a plan. I'm good with whatever you want to make. You're the chef, not me." Joel leaned in for a kiss.

Nipping Joel's lips back, Logan nuzzled his mouth. "Ooh, free rein. I like that option." He freed himself from Joel's gentle grip, gathered their coffee cups, and went to the kitchen. "Let's see what masterpiece I can create from this mess."

Joel chuckled.

Logan strutted around the kitchen. Running a finger against a perfectly clean countertop, he rubbed his fingers together. "Such a horrible work condition. I canna work in such horrid kitchen," he joked around with his lover. His attempt at a fake French accent failed. He had to grin, his fake accent truly was horrible.

"What is wrong with my kitchen? I created it with the finest materials. Top of the line appliances." Joel leaned against said 'horrid' counter and gave Logan a mock glare.

"'Dis is top-of-the-line?" Logan waved a hand around. "I've seen better, used better. I canna be sure I can create masterpieces of art in this type of environment."

"Art or food, chef?"

"Never tease the one who feeds your stomach," Logan warned.

"Rightly so," Joel said, laughing.

Shaking his head, Logan laughed with him.

In complete reality, Logan never felt happier to be in a regular kitchen and not under the hot bright lights and multiple cameras of a studio at the network. He didn't have to worry about remembering any type of lines, whether things were cooking properly, or if the recipe was going to work at that moment. Then there were all the issues of figuring out who placed what where and if the instrument he needed in the right cabinet or drawer. Unlike in his restaurants, he didn't know if the ingredients were fresh or dried. The constant pressure of living up to the reality of being the hottest new star and face of the food channel and pushed in every direction dragged and destroyed his energy. There was the constant prodding towards this place, another contract shoved under his nose to sign, the orders to join a different show as a 'guest chef' and no time in between everything. No matter how the schedule worked, he barely had five minutes to get whatever he needed. It drove him crazy.

It was madness.

While the two different shows were complete successes and took up a lot of time, he lost some control over the restaurants he loved. Sure, he was in the process of opening new branches, but he couldn't personally oversee everything like he used to. He delegated things more and more and found himself losing control.

Unless stuck in the kitchen on set, he rarely stepped into an actual kitchen and let himself free to cook whatever he wanted. He didn't have the time to play around with ingredients.

The love of cooking waned. The thought of hating the one thing he loved scared him.

It was why he took off on his motorcycle. No word to anyone. No note to anyone. Not even a damn text or email. Nothing.

He escaped the city after filming the last of the holiday episodes and shows and disappeared. His cell phone turned off and still shoved deep in the backpack along with his laptop. He may turn it on later, but not when things were going so well with Joel.

"You are a thousand miles away from me," Joel said. His voice snapped Logan out of his thoughts.

Shaking his head, Logan blinked and looked up from the cutting board where he sliced and chopped a pile of vegetables. "What?"

"Where did you go while doing all that chopping? You're damn good with that knife. I would have chopped something off if I lost my concentration."

"Years of training and practice," Logan said with a shrug. "Just wondering about how I ended up here."

"You drove into a blizzard on a motorcycle. That's how." Joel leaned over the counter and snatched a piece of carrot.

"Smart aleck." Logan smacked Joel's fingers with a wooden spoon.

"Ow!"

"Wait for dinner."

"Just a measly carrot. What's dinner?"

"Roast chicken and vegetables."

"Ooh... Sounds yummy."

"Simplified with chicken breasts to make it faster." Logan turned to heat a sauté pan for the vegetables. "How's the decorating?"

"All done while you were off in your mind. Before you ask, I put the tubs away."

"Impressive." Logan turned while the pan preheated and stepped out of the kitchen to look around. He gave a low whistle and nodded. "Now the place feels like the holidays."

"No presents though."

"Eh, who needs them? We have each other. It wouldn't be the first Christmas I didn't open a gift."

"Works for me. Need my help with anything?"

"Set the table. Can you make a new batch of iced tea?"

"Of course and I use actual leaves, not a powder," Joel said.

Catching Joel's attempt to be proud of the simple act, Logan indulged him. "Impressive."

They worked in comfortable silence while Logan sautéed the vegetables until they were softened, darkened, and released juices and aromas. He added them to the roasting pan around the prepared chicken breasts. Tossing in some additional ingredients, he covered the pan with tinfoil and stuck it in a hot oven for the rest of the needed time. Turning to clean up the workspace, he saw Joel beat him to it by wiping down the last bit with a towel.

"Well now, you're fast," Logan said.

"You're cooking, I better do the cleaning." Joel nodded toward the pan. "You done with that?"

"Yeah, leave the spoon for later."

Sliding against Logan while reaching for the pan, Joel placed a kiss on Logan's nape. He set the hot pan in the water, added a little more soap, and let it soak for a bit.

"What is left?"

"Nothing," Joel said. "Table set and tea made. I can toss together a mean salad, if you'd like."

"You can make it for yourself. I'm not allowed fresh salad," Logan said.

"Why not?"

"Poor belly can't handle it." Logan patted his belly. "Learned about ten years ago that I have IBS. To stay away from the pain and damaging symptoms, I completely changed my diet. It actually influenced a lot of what I do in the restaurants."

"Ouch, I know that stuff. Are you okay with us having sex?"

Stepping over, Logan took Joel in his arms. He kissed him deep. "As long as we're careful and my system is calm and healthy, yes. Right now, I have things under control and my diet is good. I have to deal with stress more than anything."

"Is that why you took off on your bike?"

"It was hectic, to say the least."

"What about your restaurants? Aren't you needed in the kitchens?"

"Part of my current problem is that I lost a lot of hands-on work with them the last couple of years. Guess I've hit a crossroads and I need to figure out what I want to do with my life. Continue the path I'm going now, or return to my first love with the restaurants."

"What do you want to happen?"

"Combination of both and more. I'm greedy. I love both aspects of my life, but lately it's all consuming. Working eighteen hour days, seven days a week, always on the go, surrounded by people, everyone wants a piece of the pie."

"Sounds like you're a celebrity," Joel said, stepping back to the other counter. "Is there something you're not telling me?"

Logan glanced at his newfound lover, shoved a frustrated hand through his hair. "Crap, I didn't want all my issues to come up. I wanted this time to pass without that side of me entering into this bit of haven I found with you."

"Why is that?"

"You know nothing about that upfront side of me. You don't expect anything from me. It's relaxing, Joel. You see me as me, Logan, plain ordinary Logan, standing here in front of you. I don't have to keep a wall up to protect myself from you." Logan opened his arms and banged a fist against his chest. "This Logan and you want me for this Logan and nothing else. Just the idiot who drove a motorcycle into a blizzard and fell into your arms at Christmas."

Staying quiet, Joel listened to his rant and pleas.

"Can I stay this Logan for a little longer? Please. As my Christmas present?"

Joel pulled in a deep breath and released it. "You're not some married guy looking for a fix or something? Are you?"

Logan cracked up laughing and shook his head. "Hell no. Just a lonely gay guy who has a hectic life."

"All right. If it turns out different, you're getting tossed in the snow."

"On my honor, if you find out anything horrible, you have my permission to toss me sans clothes into the snow." Logan held his hand up and gave him the Boy Scout's pledge.

"Good." Joel glanced at him. "You'll tell me what's going on later. Right?"

"If you want to know, I will, but after Christmas."

"If we want to go for more than beyond the fling," Joel added. "But the plan is still to walk away without regrets after the holiday."

Logan wasn't sure if this would remain a simple 'fling' where he could walk away without a look back. His heart thumped hard at the foray into reality. Logan released a long breath and hoped he didn't screw things up with Joel. He turned and checked on their dinner.

During a lazy, sensual morning spent in bed, they learned every inch of each other's bodies, nuzzled, and cuddled. Both of them grateful Joel stashed a box of condoms in the bathroom. Logan never thought he would turn into someone who loved to snuggle.

Rising when their bellies grumbled and complained, Logan created them a delicious breakfast of French toast with the works. He finished the mulled cider and batches of cookies. Recipes flipped through his mind while he studied the ingredients to begin pulling together a Christmas dinner for two.

Joel disappeared to work in the woodshop. He mentioned something about putting in some time on the hutch project.

An easy camaraderie fell between them, each concentrated on their own projects. Logan had never felt more content than he did in that moment.

A lot of that contentment was due to Joel and their sexual connection, but it felt deeper than sex. Something down to the soul.

Logan didn't know if this continued to be just a holiday fling. At least on his side.

He was only kidding himself. He couldn't see a way for him to stay here with Joel and still return to his life in the city and in front of the camera for *In Logan's Kitchen*. Everyone wanted to cook with the hottest gay chef around and get a piece of him.

Trouble was there weren't any pieces left of him to give.

Letting out a troubled sigh, Logan turned to the oven as the timer dinged. Opening the door, he pulled out the last batch of sugar cookies and placed it on the hot pad. He slid in a tray filled with chocolate chip cookies.

"Damn, it smells delicious in here. I smell chocolate chip cookies. What else are you creating?" Joel entered the room from the workshop. He closed the door behind him to seal out the cold. He wrapped his arms around Logan.

Logan shivered and yipped when a cold nose and chin nuzzled his warm neck. "You're freezing!"

"You smell delicious," Joel teased. "Like cinnamon and chocolate. Yum!"

Laughing, Logan twisted to plant a kiss on Joel's lips. "That's what you get for playing with your wood piles. Get a mug of cider. It should be ready by now."

"Cider?"

"Mulled cider."

"Damn, it's been a while since I've had some of that." Joel moved away after stealing a few more kisses and ladled a full mug. Taking a few careful sips, he grinned and nodded. "Perfect. Sugar cookies too?"

"Chocolate chip cookies are in the works, which you smelled. I figured you can enjoy them as a treat."

"You're a baking fiend."

"I get in that type of mood around the holidays. Usually, I never have the time to indulge myself. I'm making up for it now."

"Are we having cookies for dinner? Not that I mind." Joel leaned against the counter while he munched on a cookie.

"No, I can do a little better than cookies for dinner. I'm making full use of your double ovens for probably the first time since you put them in, correct?"

Joel shrugged.

"I have a turkey roasting to perfection."

"Turkey? There was a turkey in the freezer?"

"I found a good-sized turkey. You ordered a full bird. Did you forget about it?"

"Guess I did."

"I'm making use of it. I decided on stuffing, sweet potatoes, and roasted carrots. They'll go in when I'm done with the cookies. I should have time to whip up a round of biscuits."

"You're handy to have in the kitchen."

"You definitely won't go hungry. Depending on how much we eat, you should have plenty of leftovers to last you for a while. Lots of carved turkey sandwiches." Logan patted a hand against Joel's flat abdomen on his way to open the oven when the timer dinged. "Out of my way, please."

A loud bang thumped against the mudroom door.

"What the hell?" Joel muttered and went to see what happened.

"Perhaps the blizzard knocked over something. Check on my baby, please."

"Yeah, yeah, I'll make sure things are tied down. Last time I checked, things were starting to clear when I came in from the shop."

"Really? That's surprising, but never can tell with this weather."

"Holy hell, what are you doing here?" Joel called out.

"Merry Christmas Eve! Surprise! We didn't want you to be alone tonight, so we trudged on over, bringing the party to you."

Logan stopped in mid-motion of putting the next batch of cookies in the oven at the sounds of multiple voices echoed in the mudroom with Joel's baritone. He didn't expect anyone would face a blizzard, even on Christmas Eve, to get to a party, especially when there wasn't one.

"Wow!" someone called out. "Do you smell that?"

"Yeah, I do," another person answered.

"Damn, it smells delicious in here. Fresh baked cookies and mulled cider mixed in with Christmas tree. Since I know you can't cook, that must be some realistic set of candles you're burning, Joel. Where can I get some of those?" one of the guests called out.

"They're not candles, Allan, nor am I alone. I have someone here..." Joel entered the kitchen, followed by four others.

Sticking the tray in the oven and closing it, Logan set the timer and turned to face the unexpected crowd of Joel's friends. He smiled and waved a hand.

"Ohmigod!" one of the two women screamed. "It's him... it's you..."

"It's who, Shannon?" Joel asked with a confused look on his face as the two women gushed and squeaked.

Logan closed his eyes. This moment he dreaded would happen. The little bubble of happiness popped before his eyes. Reality set in. His perfect quiet holiday came to a bitter end.

"The hottest chef on TV, even if he's gay. Oh, wow, Logan McNair. I watch you all the time! I can't believe you're here." Shannon rushed over to clasp his arm.

Logan backtracked until the countertop dug into his back. He shot Joel a frantic look.

"Hey, hey, Shannon, back off from him. Please. Can someone tell me what is happening?" Joel followed and stopped. "Chef? TV?"

Shannon stopped and looked between Logan and Joel.

"Duh! Forgot you don't have television. This is Logan McNair of the show *In Logan's Kitchen. The* Logan, the Gay Chef!" Shannon and Maria screeched together.

Logan winced.

"Has he been here all this time? The news and gossip channels are going crazy about your disappearance, Mr. McNair. They swear something bad happened to you." Maria swiveled around her husband, Allan, to get to Logan.

Logan leaned back again.

"Maria, Shannon, stop, please don't corner him." Joel entered the kitchen and got between him and Joel.

"But... He's the Gay Chef!" Maria argued.

"He's still just a regular man, Maria, and should be treated the exact same way," Joel demanded.

Logan relaxed a tiny bit behind Joel's protection. He wrapped his fingers around a loop on Joel's jeans. He didn't say a word, not to the ladies or Joel. He didn't want to see Joel's face and reaction to the truth.

"Maria, Shannon, Joel is right. Back up and leave Logan alone. Come on, get on the other side of the countertop. He's Joel's guest and friend. Give him some damn breathing room," Allan said. "Greg, give me a hand."

"Shannon, you heard Joel and Allan. Back off," the fourth guest said, clearing his throat while fixing his wire-rimmed glasses. "I'm sorry about that, Mr. McNair, Shannon is a huge fan. She has all your books and DVR's your shows."

"Let's start this all over, shall we?" Joel stepped forward, away from Logan, who let go of the loop when the women left the kitchen. He glanced back at Logan and his friends. He moved to the side to keep everyone in view. "Seems there's some explaining to do."

Shannon looked between them. "He didn't tell you about himself?"

"No, Shannon, Logan didn't say anything other than he's a chef with a couple of restaurants. We wanted to keep the outside world back. I promised Logan I wouldn't demand more answers." Joel crossed arms over his chest and glanced to Logan. "Looks like that's about to change, huh, Logan?"

Logan gripped the back of his neck in uneasiness and disappointment that his quiet time with Joel disappeared. It had only been wishful thinking. He could only nod.

Chapter 8

After settling everyone around the dining table with mugs of mulled cider and a plate of fresh cookies, Logan leaned against the counter, to keep an eye on the remaining cookies, dinner, and his distance.

Joel remained next to him and not his guests. "I'm not angry. Go ahead and say what you want to them." He drew his knuckles down Logan's side. He kept their conversation low and private between them.

Logan concentrated on the pot next to him and nowhere else. "Didn't want you to react..."

"Like them?"

Logan nodded.

"I'm not. I know the real you, Logan, the one behind the celebrity," Joel said.

"It's only been a couple of days."

"I know enough about you to make my opinion. Celebrity status is cool, but not necessary."

"Thanks," Logan said.

Joel bumped their shoulders together. "You don't have to tell them anything. It's up to you."

"Good to get it out. Tell you everything too."

Joel glanced at his friends. "Okay. You can ask Logan questions, but don't spit all of them out at once."

"Why did you disappear from L.A.? Why did you come here? Out of all places," Maria asked.

"Maria," her husband said.

"It's all one type of question," she said and shushed him with her hands.

"It's been such a big mystery. A top story," Shannon added.

"Logan..." Joel placed a hand on Logan's shoulder.

Blowing out a long breath, knowing it was best to get it all out, Logan stirred the contents of a dish. Then he took a bracing sip of cider. "After wrapping the last holiday special, I took off without a word to anyone. I needed a break from things. Knowing everyone, including my agent, would try to prevent me from leaving, I didn't tell them. Packed my stuff on my motorcycle and took off for my cabin, which is down the lake from Joel. When I got there, I found it trashed from my younger brother's uninvited partying."

"That group of wild partiers? That was your brother's group?" Greg said.

"Yeah, I changed the locks and moved the keys, but somehow he found them. I apologize for the trouble they caused. If there's other damage, I'll make sure it's fixed and covered."

Greg raised a hand and shook his head. "Other than a noise nuisance, they kept to the cabin."

"Yeah, not sure what I'm going to do about the cabin," Logan said.

"It's a disaster area," Joel added.

"What happened when you got to the cabin?" Shannon asked to pick up the story.

"Joel found me in my unfortunate predicament since he's kept an eye on the place and did his loop of checks around the lake. He stopped at my cabin last and found me," Logan said.

"Wait a minute." Allan held up a hand. "You rode a motorcycle through a blizzard?"

A lopsided grin curled Logan's lips. "It wasn't a blizzard when I started."

Everyone chuckled at his hopeful try to ease things.

"But, yes, that's what I did. Nearly froze off some manly pieces in the process."

"Ouch," Shannon said with a girlish giggle.

"So, our darling Joel came to your rescue and you've been here since?" Maria finished the story to its natural conclusion.

"Yup." Logan glanced to Joel and grinned. "Keeping him well fed too."

"Had to get something out of the rescue," Joel said.

"That can't be all you were doing?" Maria teased.

Allan nudged her side and they whispered a variety of hushed words to each other. Until she finally kissed him hard.

"Hush, honey, Joel knows and loves us. I can see the change in him. There's a sparkle in his eyes," Maria said.

Trying hard not to glance at the other couples, Logan lowered his hand and brushed it against Joel's hip. He kept the touch private and out of view. Joel nudged him back.

"There's not much else to say. That's the story. Nothing crazy or suicidal," Logan said, adding a shrug. "I'm an overworked TV chef needing a desperate break from the rat race."

"And falling for a hunky carpenter in the process?" Shannon asked with a wink at Joel.

"Let's not go quite that far," Joel said. "I didn't play too big of a role in things. Logan did a lot on his own."

"Oh, I wouldn't put it like that. I was pretty desperate when you found me." Logan glanced down at the counter, then over at his lover. He wondered how Joel was processing in everything he learned. He wouldn't explain everything about his life in the city or his time as the Gay Chef to all of them. That would come later tonight when they were alone. He owed Joel that much after everything that happened between them. Nor did he want to tell everything to these virtual strangers.

"I see a sparkle in our Joel's eyes," Maria said.

"Okay, enough, enough," Joel said. "Yes, I took Logan to my bed. So there, it's out. So what?"

Logan turned and stared at Joel. He raised his eyebrows in surprise.

"What? I'm not ashamed of having you as my lover. Are you?"

"Hell, no," Logan said with a grin.

Joel leaned over, threaded fingers through Logan's hair, and tugged him in for a long, luscious kiss in front of his friends who whooped and cheered as the kiss went on for a few minutes longer than necessary. Logan hung on to Joel's broad shoulders until they broke apart, but he soaked in the warmth seeping from Joel's gaze.

"There, done. It's out. Get over it." Joel brushed his hands off, of cookie crumbs and the whole mess. "What's next?"

Logan shook his head and worked through the haze of the kiss. "The ground back under my feet?"

Everyone cracked up laughing at how Joel dealt with the news and Logan's reaction.

Hours later, with help from the ladies, they put a slightly larger Christmas Eve feast than Logan first planned on the table. Ecstatic at the thought of cooking with Logan, Shannon and Maria jumped at the chance to help him when he realized he needed to expand on the simple meal he started.

"Good thing the turkey went in early and is almost ten pounds. If it was smaller or just a breast, things could have been dicey. I planned for a lot of leftovers for Joel to enjoy the next week or more," Logan said with a chuckle.

"Nah, you would pull out a little chef miracle," Shannon said, full of complete pride and support for his skills.

"Or we would wait a little longer to eat and not care one whit. It's Christmas. Time to sit back, chill out, and enjoy the time with friends." Greg helped carry one of the dishes to the table.

"It's a damn good thing I put in that extra order or we'd all be screwed," Joel said. The wry comment made everyone laugh with his pessimistic attitude.

"You would be amazed at what I can create from staples," Logan said.

Leaning down, Joel kissed Logan's temple. "Thank you for cooking a wonderful Christmas Eve feast, Logan. Even when you're trying to have a holiday off."

"Here here, to the chef!" Allan cried out. He raised a glass of white wine. "A Christmas toast to our chef and the dinner he created."

The others seconded the toast.

"Thank you, everyone. It's not work around friends, and this—" He motioned to the cozy table and nice group of folks. "This type of set-up I don't mind at all." Logan picked up his glass by the stem and added to the toast. He clinked glasses with Joel. "Joel, please carve so we can serve and eat." He pointed to the head of the table to his lover.

"Are you sure?"

"Do you know how to carve a bird?" Logan raised an eyebrow.

"In wood," Joel said with a grin. He held out the carving fork and knife set and wiggled them a bit. "It's all yours, Chef."

"Oh, dear. Is he this bad around all kinds of food?" Logan returned to the head of the table, nudged Joel aside, and accepted the carving fork and knife.

"The man boils soup dry," Maria said.

Logan stared at her, his jaw dropped. "Tell me you're kidding."

She shook her head.

Logan looked at Joel. "Do I need to give you lessons?"

"Will that keep you around longer? I can be a really bad student to keep you around," Joel teased.

Shaking his head at Joel's teasing and his earlier dream about figuring out a way to stay, Logan carved his way through the bird. Joel and his friends teased each other about simple, everyday things. He missed this kind of conversation amongst his table in the city. Everything there was the latest gossip, money, the newest show or gig, or some other type of drama.

What life would he choose? The city one where he had a hit show and restaurants or the quiet valley filled with life and love.

His Christmas Eve wish.

Chapter 9

Lying on top of the covers, the fireplace crackled merrily behind him the only source of light and heat in the cabin, Joel settled down on the mattress next to Logan. Both only wore sweatpants. After hours of talking, cleaning up, laughter, and games with more cookies and cider, the unexpected party lasted longer than anyone planned. Things didn't break up until the wee hours of Christmas morning. Their guests finally bundled up against the weather and headed home. Leaving the couple alone.

"Sorry about all that craziness. I didn't think anyone would try to push through a blizzard to visit," Joel said.

"Your friends are wonderful, Joel. I enjoyed spending the time with them, more than I have in a long time." Logan stretched out a hand and ran it over Joel's strong thigh, felt the muscle quiver under his touch.

"Why didn't you tell me the truth?"

Fearing this would come up, Logan let out a sigh. "You saw how your friends reacted to me. I'm a celebrity to most people, coming into their homes via the television every day for an hour or more. To some, they think they know who I am, that I'm their best friend and they know everything about me. The reaction varies, but I never know if it's for me, the plain everyday Logan, or Logan the Gay Chef. It's kind of hard to tell."

"Even worse in personal circumstances?"

"Ten-times worse, and I've been burned. Hell, I've been scorched." Logan dropped flat on his back, draped an arm over his eyes. "It's only gotten nastier as the TV series increased with the *Gay Chef* and then *In Logan's Kitchen* created, the cookbooks, the restaurants, now they want a magazine deal. I'm losing so much..."

"But gaining at the same time."

"I don't know who I am anymore, Joel. When I started, all I wanted was to own my own restaurant and create meals everyone enjoyed. I didn't plan for some producer to visit my restaurant, enjoy a meal, and demand to meet me. He talked me into auditioning for a show, to see if they could build something around me. I certainly didn't expect it to take off and become almost meteoric."

"Logan..."

Feeling Joel tugging on his arm, Logan let him move it. He opened his eyes and stared at his lover, found in a blizzard, who'd captured his soul in a few days due to his simple ways. In the warm firelight, he saw the gentle warmth in the lake blue gaze. He leaned into the calloused touch of Joel's fingers and nuzzled them.

"Tell me what happened to you."

"I lost my center, my rock. There's no support to keep me centered and grounded. I have people pushing me in different directions, telling me where to go, what I must do every moment of the day. There are general scripts to remember, setting up the different components to make the show go smoother. Then there is all the promo I need to do or a visit on another show. Things are non-stop, no breaks, no down time. I have no place to go that's mine."

"The cabin?"

"Thanks to Malcolm, it's gone. Still, the past three or five years, I couldn't get away from L.A. to stay a few days. I don't know if it's even worth it to rebuild it."

"What are you trying to tell me?"

"I don't know what I'm saying," Logan said. His voice broke with a bit of fear and pain. "Until I cooked here, I had a severe lack of enthusiasm when it came to cooking. There were moments when I didn't want to cook or be a chef anymore. Those moments increased over the last year."

"Hey, hey, it's okay to feel lost. It's okay." Joel soothed him with his touch and voice. "I felt it too before I found my direction again. It's why I left the flipping houses business and came here, built the cabin and my new life. I had no idea if it would work."

Tears welled in Logan's eyes. He squeezed them shut. "It's getting to be too much for me. Too fast. Too hard. Two shows. So many restaurants. Five cookbooks, with three more scheduled. Now they want to add in a magazine. A magazine! What the hell next? A frigging talk show?" Logan opened his eyes and stared at Joel. "I'm not the answer to all gay men! I don't have all the answers. I enjoy cooking, damn it. That's it! Put me in a kitchen and let me be!"

"Then tell them that!"

"I did! They laughed and said I'll get over it, it'll pass." Logan shrugged. "Now I don't even want to step into a kitchen. At least one on the set."

Sitting up, Joel gathered Logan and pulled him against him. He rocked him with a tenderness.

Logan clung to him, wrapped his arms around Logan's strong shoulders. "It's why after the holiday shooting finished, I packed up and disappeared. I couldn't handle it any longer. I needed to escape the cage, the pressure."

"Calls or emails?"

"Don't know. Phone and laptop are off and in the backpack."

"You haven't opened either one?"

"Too damn scared about what new can of crap I'll open. Guess that's why there's all those scary stories on the television about my disappearance."

"Shit, Logan, you can't run away from your life. Not like that. You need to tell them you're okay. At least give them that."

"Then they'll try to come and find me. They'll drag me back before I'm ready to go."

"You can't be afraid of that happening."

"Why can't I be afraid?" Logan pulled back. "I can't live like that. Not anymore. It's not living. It's barely surviving. I told you how I was beginning to hate cooking. Me. I didn't want to be standing in a kitchen, dealing with food, creating a delicious meal."

Leaning back, Joel framed Logan's face and made him meet his gaze. "What do you want, Logan McNair? Deep down in your heart, what do you want?"

"Oh man, there's so much," Logan said.

"Tell me. List it all out. In the open."

"I want to love being in a kitchen again, enjoy working with ingredients. I can create something I know another person will love and adore when they place it in their mouth. I would love to breathe and control what I want to do with my career. I want..."

"Go on..."

"I want love in my life," Logan whispered. "I don't want a fling. I want a soul deep relationship with love, with you, Joel."

"Well, thank Christmas and that damn blizzard for that last bit."

Logan's eyebrows rose.

Joel ran his hand up and down Logan's back, before threading his fingers through Logan's hair. He cupped his hand around Logan's neck and brought their heads together. Their gazes met and went soul deep. "Did you think you were going to leave my cabin that easily?"

Logan blinked, fought back tears at the gentle touch of his lover. "I hoped you weren't going to let me go."

"Made a crazy Christmas wish to keep you forever in my arms, silly man." Joel grinned and shrugged. He kissed his lover long and deep. "I love you something crazy, blizzard chef."

"Blizzard chef?"

"The perfect combination about how I found you and what you are. It fits you, my Logan. Looks like my wish is going to come true. I didn't want to go hungry and you didn't want to go lonely. The rest of your problems we'll figure out together. After the holidays."

Framing Joel's beloved face with his hands, Logan stared long and deep and smiled. "Looks like we both get our Christmas wishes."

The End

Nicole Dennis

Dreamy...Sensual...Forever Love

A quiet one, Nicole Dennis is the penname of an asexual author of different genres of fiction – both LGBT+ and hetero. Lots of characters, worlds, and stories build up in her head until she must get them down on the screen – anything from romance to fantasy to paranormal.

During the day, she works in a quiet office in Central Florida, where she makes her home, and enjoys the down time to slip into her imagination. A feline companion owns her – a fluffy house panther, known as Midnight the Void. An incredibly special furbaby who is FIV+ and polydactyl on her front paws (fluffy danger mittens!).

Contact & Media Info:

Website: http://nicoledennis.net

Email: nicoledennis.author@gmail.com

Facebook:

Main: www.facebook.com/NicoleDennis.Author

Page: https://www.facebook.com/NicoleDennis.Musings/

Group: https://www.facebook.com/groups/nicoledennis.author/

Amazon: https://www.amazon.com/author/nicoledennis

Threads: https://www.threads.net/@ndennis_author

Mastodon: https://mastodon.lol/@nicoledennis

QueeRomance: https://www.queeromanceink.com/mbm-book-author/nicole-dennis/

Goodreads: http://www.goodreads.com/author/show/2791975.Nicole_Dennis

. . . .

CURRENT BOOKS:

Entwined Publishing / Enticed/Pride Publishing
Southern Charm Series
1 – Rules of the Chef
2 – By the Numbers
3 – On the Green
4 – When in Bloom
5 – Following the Law
6 – According to Design
7 – Unexpected in the End (Coming 2025)
Freebies available on my website or email for PDF
Mischief Corner Books:
Secrets & Silk
Siren Publishing: (BookStrand.com)
Grant's Mechanic (MM)
Unholy Angel (MF Erotic Paranormal)
Fire Jaguars (MMF Paranormal)
1 – Fire Moon Dance
2 – Luna Moon Dance
3 – Dark Moon Dance
Other books are in the works
FatCat Books Ink (Self-Pub home):
New Stories:
Lyon Lynx Clan
Paws in the Snow (Prequel)
McShayne Bloodline
1 – McShayne's Dragon
2 – McShayne's Fae
3 – McShayne's Elf
4 – McShayne's Merman (Coming 2025)

Cheimon Tales

1 – Cracks in the Ice

2 – Strike's Stand (In the works)

3 – Mistletoe's Story (In the works)

Carnival of Mysteries (Multi-Author Collection)

1 – Dryad on Fire

2 – Flames of the Arcane

Re-Releases:

Walk Me Trilogy

1 – Walk Me Down the Middle

2 – Walk Me Through the Haze

3 – Walk Me Through the Darkness

7 Days of Christmas

Built Piece by Piece

At the Masquerade

A Christmas Eve Wish